PIANO SHEET MUSIC for KIDS

Book + Online Video How to Play + Online Audio Files

BEGINNER PIANO BOOK for CHILDREN

Easy Piano Arrangements with 35 Popular Children Songs in 2 Levels of Difficulty (Total 70 Songs)

Paul Terence

We like to do good deeds, so every month, 5% of
the profit from books we invest in buying food
for homeless animals and feed them.

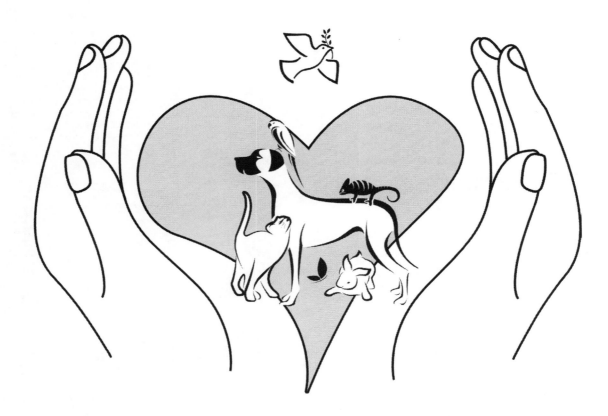

Messages about typos, errors, inaccuracies and suggestions for
improving the quality are gratefully received at:
help@paulterence.com

CONTENTS

LEVEL 1

A-Tisket, A-Tasket......6
All Through the Night......7
Alphabet Song......8
Amazing Grace......9
Baa Baa Black Sheep......10
Billy Boy......11
Bingo......12
Brother John......13
Clementine (Oh, My Darling)......14
Georgie Porgie......16
Happy Birthday......17
Hickory Dickory Dock......18
Humpty Dumpty......19
Greensleeves......20
Hush, Little Baby......22
London Bridge......23
Jingle Bells......24
Mary Had a Little Lamb......26
My Bonnie Lies Over The Ocean......27
O When The Saints......28
Old MacDonald Had a Farm......29
Pop! Goes the Weasel......30
Pussy Cat, Pussy Cat......31
Rain, Rain, Go Away......32
Shenandoah......33
Silent Night......34
Skip to My Lou......35
Simple Gifts......36
The Farmer in the Dell......38
The Muffin Man......39
This Little Light of Mine......40
This Old Man......41
Twinkle, Twinkle, Little Star......42
Yankee Doodle......43
We Wish You A Merry Christmas......44

LEVEL 2

A-Tisket, A-Tasket......46
All Through the Night......47
Alphabet Song......48
Amazing Grace......49
Baa Baa Black Sheep......50
Billy Boy......51
Bingo......52
Brother John......53
Clementine (Oh, My Darling)......54
Greensleeves......56
Georgie Porgie......58
Happy Birthday......59
Hickory Dickory Dock......60
Humpty Dumpty......61
Hush, Little Baby......62
Jingle Bells......64
London Bridge......66
Mary Had a Little Lamb......67
My Bonnie Lies Over The Ocean......68
O When The Saints......70
Old MacDonald Had a Farm......71
Pop! Goes the Weasel......72
Pussy Cat, Pussy Cat......73
Rain, Rain, Go Away......74
Shenandoah......75
Silent Night......76
Simple Gifts......78
Skip to My Lou......80
The Farmer in the Dell......82
The Muffin Man......84
This Little Light of Mine......85
This Old Man......86
Twinkle, Twinkle, Little Star......87
We Wish You A Merry Christmas......88
Yankee Doodle......90
BONUS......92

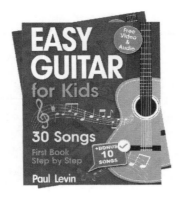

NOTES

We recommend that you practice the Level 1 songs first, then move on to Level 2.

We've also made separate printable files so you can print the song you need separately.
The song files are available in two versions:
- with and without fingering,
- with and without note names.

Links to additional materials can be found on **page 92**.

Instructions on how to use the QR code:

1 - Turn on the QR code reader application on your phone (camera, browser or other application).

2 - Point your camera at the QR code.

3 - Click on the link.

4 (video) – when the video opens, press play.

4 (audio) – when the audio window opens, press play (or download).

If you can't scan the QR code, you can enter the link manually (page 92).

In the beginning, you can play slower than the song says to make it easier. When you get better acquainted with the song, you can play it in the original tempo or even faster. Experiment with the tempo!
You can find out what the right tempo sounds like by typing in "online metronome" and enter the tempo you want, or if you already have a metronome, just set it to the right tempo.

Score	1 - and	2 - and	3 - and	4 - and			

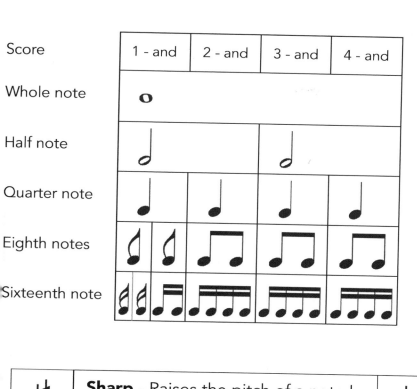

Whole rest		▬
Half rest		▬
Quarter rest		𝄽
Eighth rest		𝄾
Sixteenth rest		𝄿

♯	**Sharp** - Raises the pitch of a note by one semitone.	♭	**Flat** - Lowers the pitch of a note by one semitone.
♮	The **natural** sign in front of a music note cancels the effect of sharps and flats. Valid until the end of the bar.		

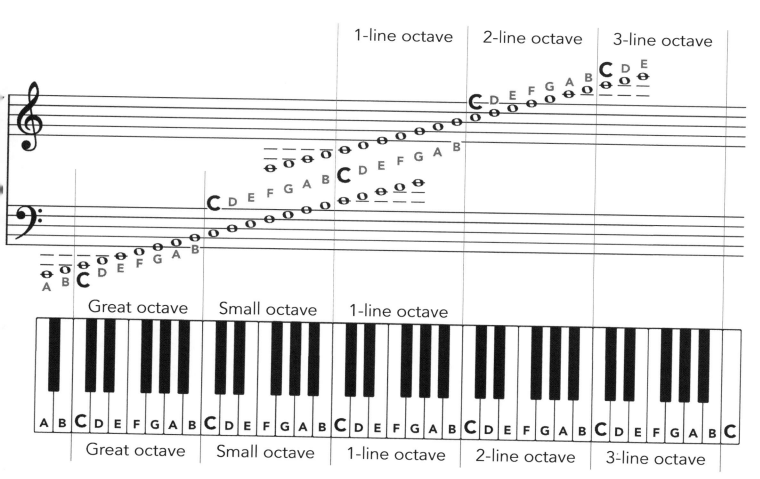

A-Tisket, A-Tasket

Children's song

Video

Audio

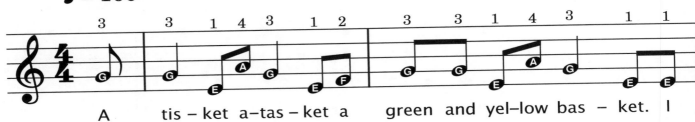

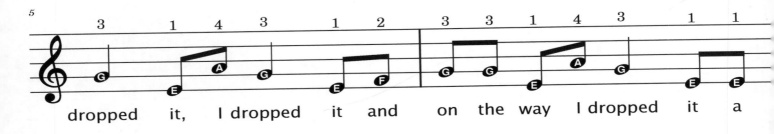

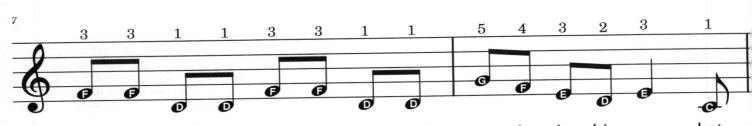

All Through the Night

Christmas carol

Audio

Video

Sleep my child and peace at-tend thee all through the night. Guard – ian an – gels God will send thee all through the night. Soft and drow-sy hours are creep-ing hill and vale in slum – ber sleep – ing. God His lov – ing vig – il keep-ing all through the night.

Alphabet Song

Children's song

Video

Audio

Level 1

Amazing Grace

Christian hymn

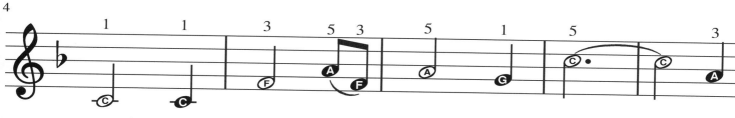

A – ma – zing   grace   how   sweet   the

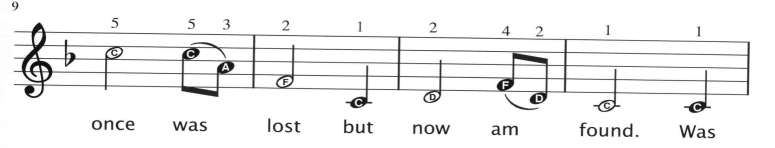

sound   that   saved   a   wretch   like   me.   I

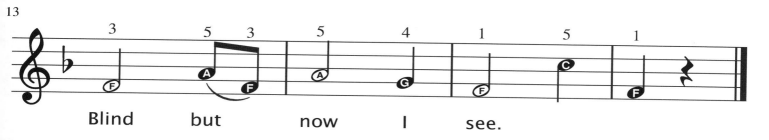

once   was   lost   but   now   am   found.   Was

Blind   but   now   I   see.

Baa Baa Black Sheep

Children's song

Audio ♩ = 120

Video

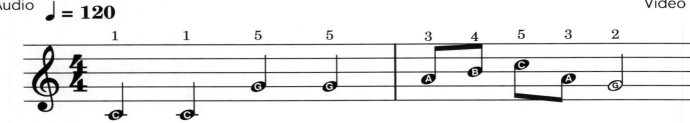

Baa, baa, black sheep have you an – y wool?

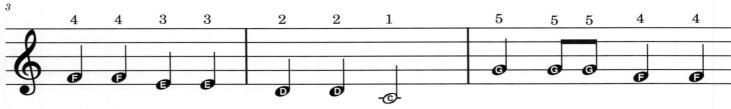

Yes sir, yes sir three bags full. One for the mast – er,

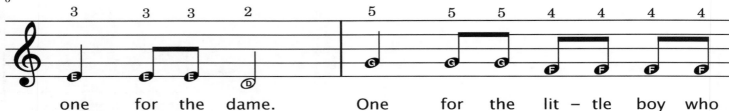

one for the dame. One for the lit – tle boy who

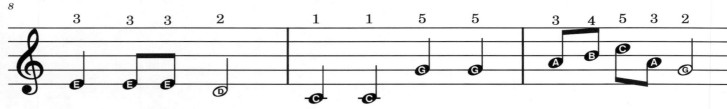

lives down the lane. Baa, baa, black sheep have you an – y wool?

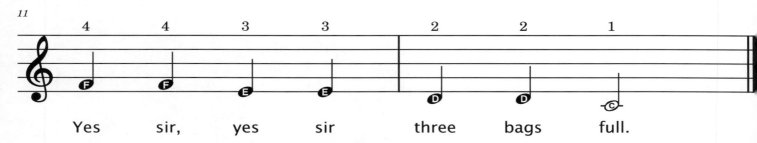

Yes sir, yes sir three bags full.

Billy Boy

Children's song

Bingo

Children's song

Audio

Video

Level 1

Brother John

Children's song

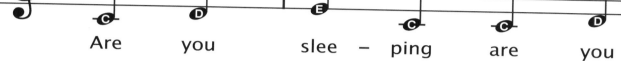

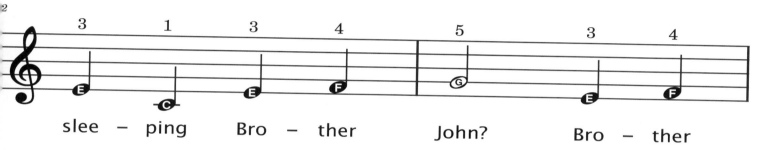

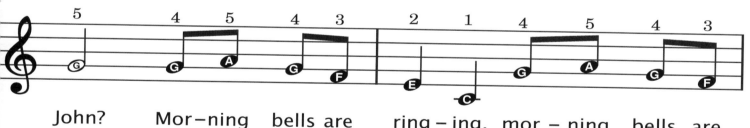

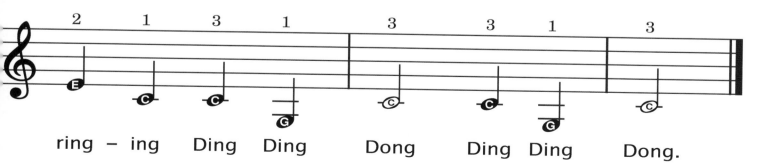

Level 1

Clementine (Oh, My Darling)

Children's song

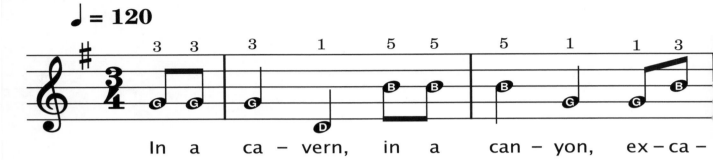

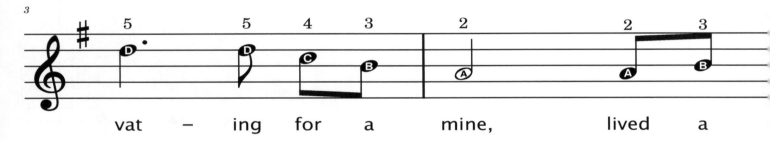

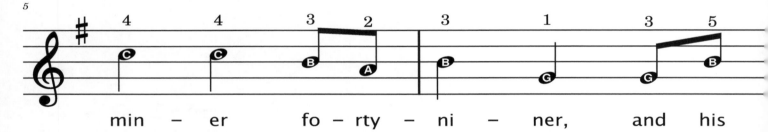

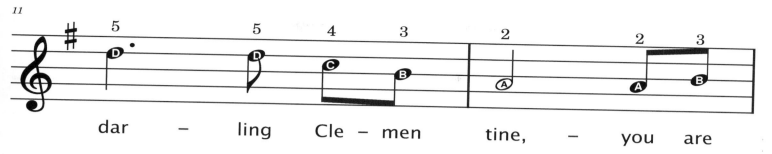

dar — ling Cle — men tine, — you are

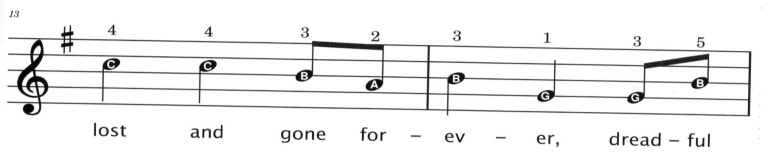

lost and gone for — ev — er, dread — ful

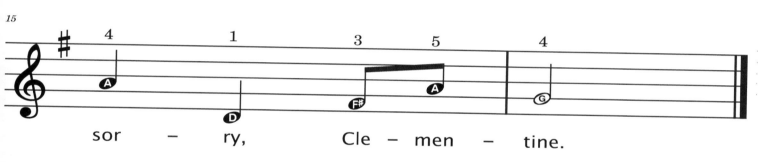

sor — ry, Cle — men — tine.

Level 1

Georgie Porgie

Children's song

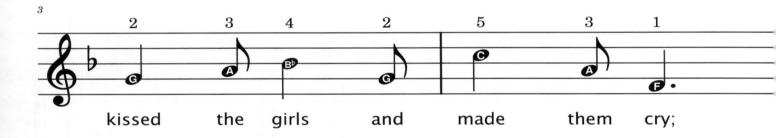

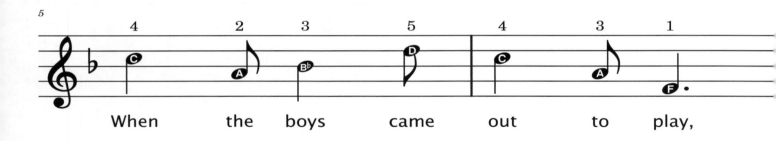

Happy Birthday

Traditional song

Video

Audio

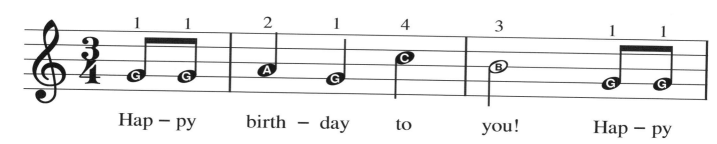

Hap – py   birth – day   to   you!   Hap – py

birth – day   to   you!   Hap – py   birth – day   de – ar

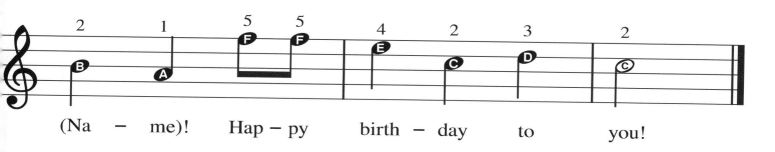

(Na – me)!   Hap – py   birth – day   to   you!

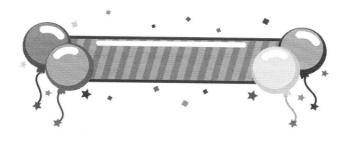

Hickory Dickory Dock

Children's song

Audio

Video

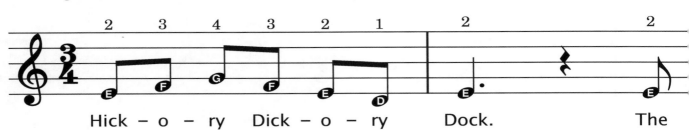

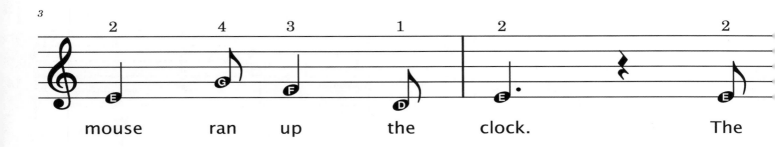

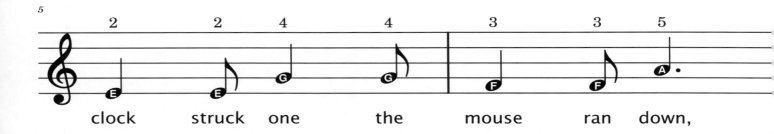

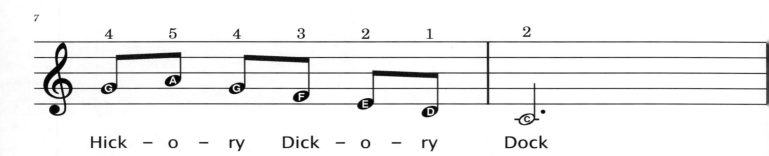

Audio

Humpty Dumpty

Children's song

Video

♩ = 110

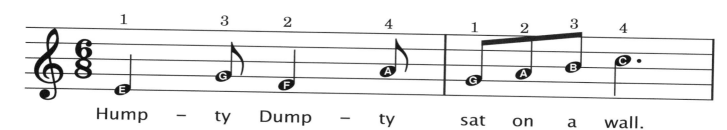

Hump – ty Dump – ty sat on a wall.

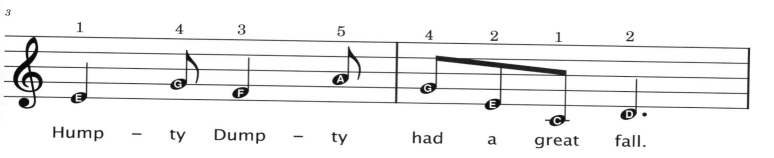

Hump – ty Dump – ty had a great fall.

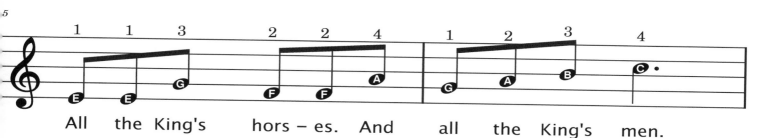

All the King's hors – es. And all the King's men.

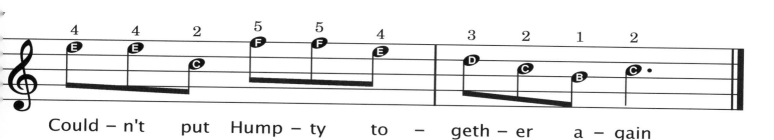

Could – n't put Hump – ty to – geth – er a – gain

Level 1

Greensleeves

English Folk Song

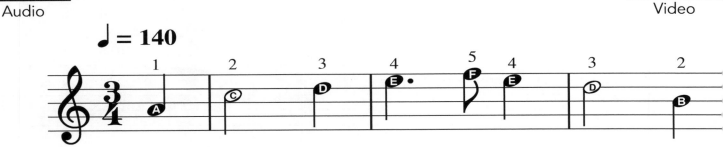

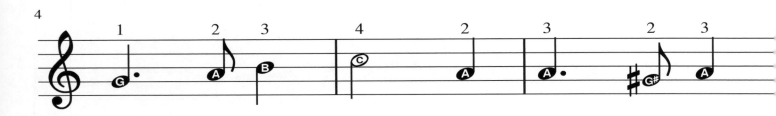

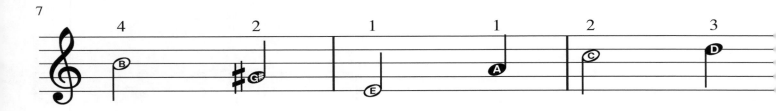

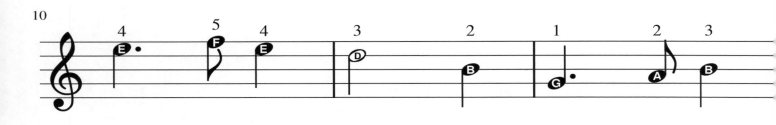

Hush, Little Baby

Children's song

♩ = 110

Hush, lit – tle ba – by don't say a word,

Pa – pa's gon–na buy you a mock–ing bird. If that mock–ing

bird don't sing, Pa–pa's gon–na buy you a dia–mond ring.

Level 1

London Bridge

Children's song

♩ = 110

4	5	4	3	2	3	4	1	2	3
G	A	G	F	E	F	G	D	E	F

Lon-don Bridge is fall-ing down, fall-ing down,

2	3	4	4	5	4	3	2	3	4
E	F	G	G	A	G	F	E	F	G

fall – ing down. Lon – don Bridge is fall-ing down,

1	4	2	1	4	5	4	3	2	3	4
D	G	E	C	G	A	G	F	E	F	G

My fair la – dy. Take a key and lock her up,

1	2	3	2	3	4	4	5	4	3	2	3	4
D	E	F	E	F	G	G	A	G	F	E	F	G

lock her up, lock lock up. Take a key and lock her up,

1	4	2	1
D	G	E	C

My fair la – dy.

2

Jingle Bells

Christmas carol

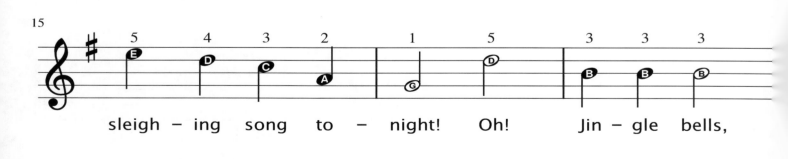

Level 1

Mary Had a Little Lamb

Children's song

Audio

Video

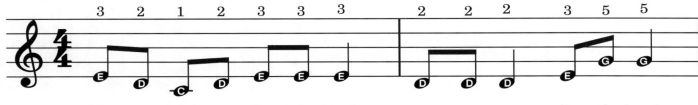

Ma – ry had a lit – tle lamb   Litt – le lamb,   lit – tle lamb.

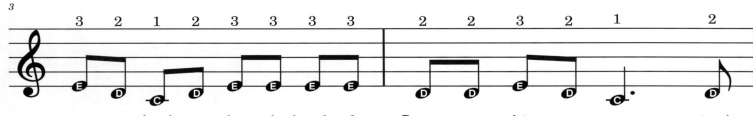

Ma – ry had a lit – tle lamb it's   fleece was white as snow.   And

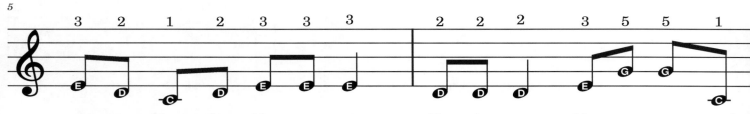

ev – ery–where that Ma – ry went,   Ma – ry went,   Ma – ry went, and

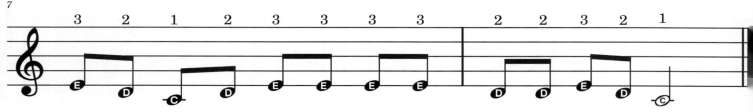

ev – ery–where that Ma – ry went, the   lamb was sure to go.

My Bonnie Lies Over The Ocean

Children's song

Audio

Video

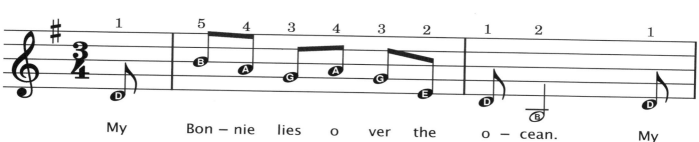

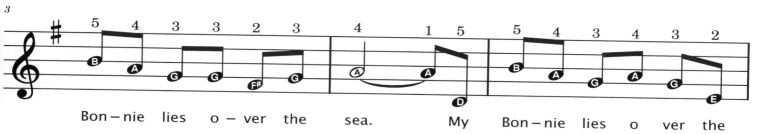

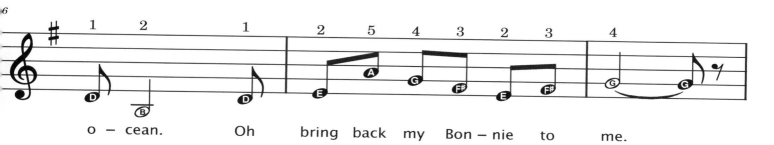

O When The Saints

Christian hymn

Audio

Video

♩ = 120

Oh when the Saints, go march–ing in. Oh when the saints go march – ing in. Oh, Lord I want to be in that num – ber when the saints go march–ing in.

Video

Level 1

Old MacDonald Had a Farm

Children's song

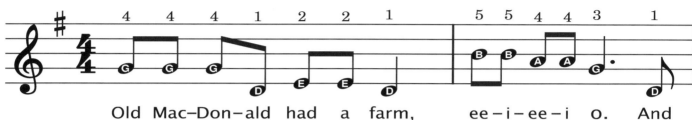

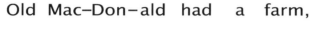

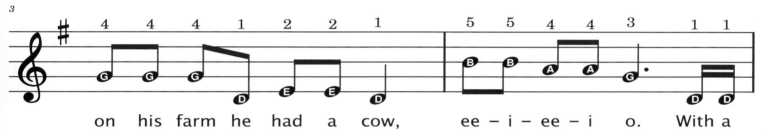

Old Mac–Don–ald had a farm, ee – i – ee – i o. And

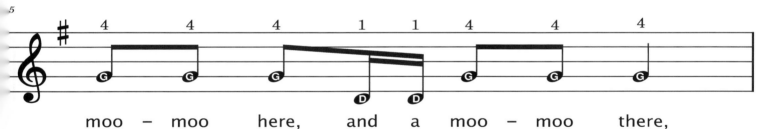

on his farm he had a cow, ee – i – ee – i o. With a

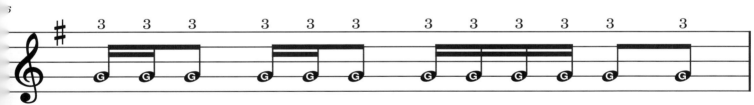

moo – moo here, and a moo – moo there,

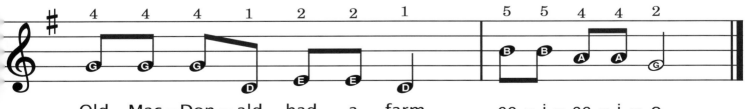

here a moo, there a moo, eve–ry–where a moo – moo

Old Mac–Don–ald had a farm, ee – i – ee – i – o.

Level 1

Pop! Goes the Weasel

Children's song

♩ = 160

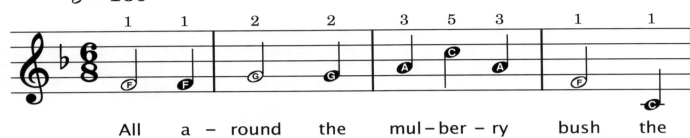

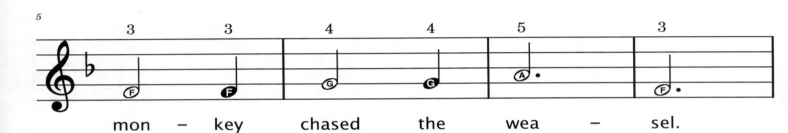

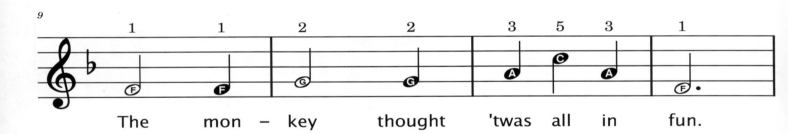

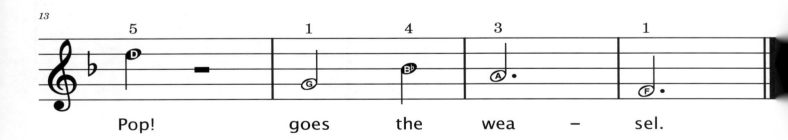

Pussy Cat, Pussy Cat

Children's song

Audio

Video

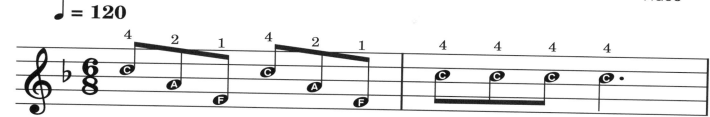

Pus – sy   cat, pus – sy   cat,   where have   you   been?

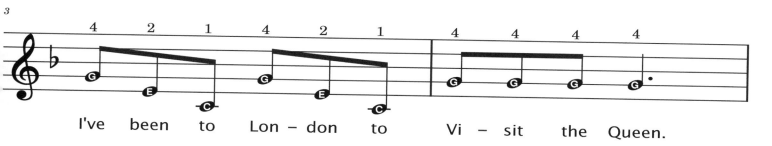

I've   been   to   Lon – don   to   Vi – sit   the   Queen.

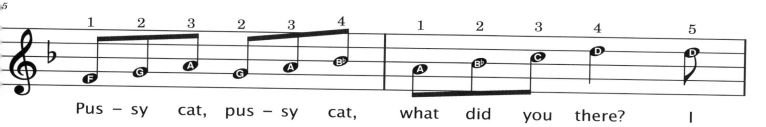

Pus – sy   cat, pus – sy   cat,   what   did   you   there?   I

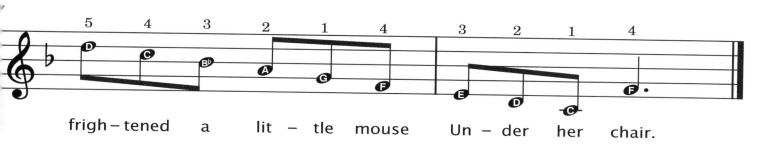

frigh – tened   a   lit – tle   mouse   Un – der   her   chair.

Level 1

Rain, Rain, Go Away

Children's song

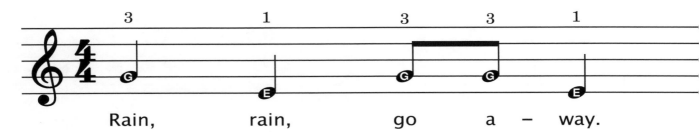

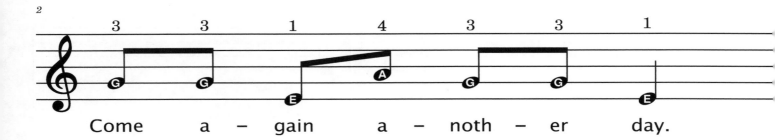

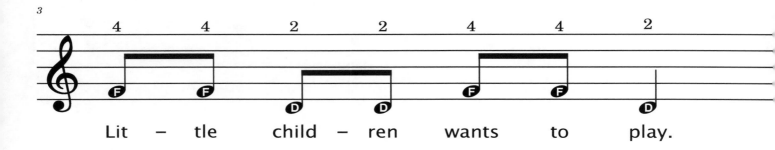

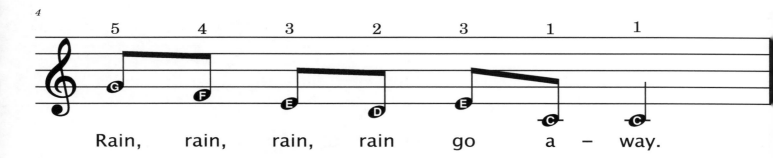

Level 1

Shenandoah

American Folk Song

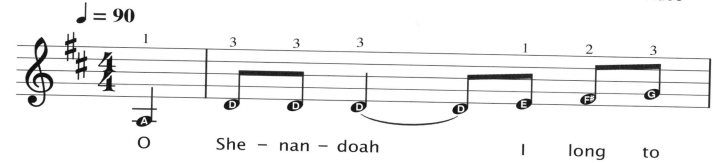

O She – nan – doah I long to

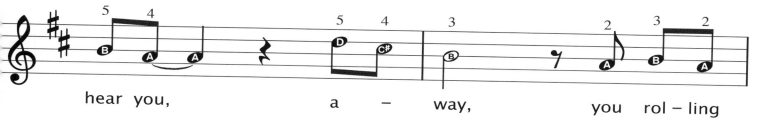

hear you, a – way, you rol – ling

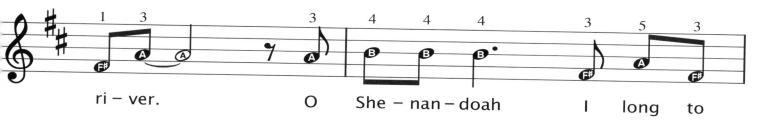

ri – ver. O She – nan – doah I long to

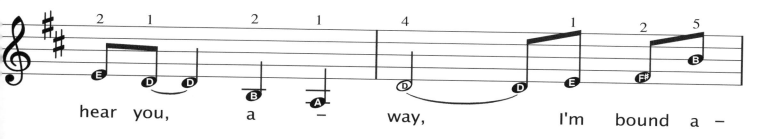

hear you, a – way, I'm bound a –

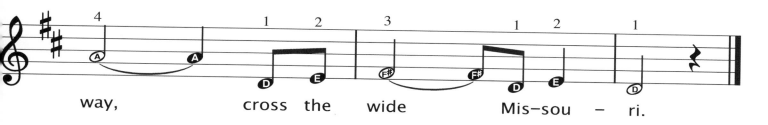

way, cross the wide Mis–sou – ri.

Silent Night

Christmas carol

Audio

Video

♩ = 120

Si – lent night, Ho – ly night! All is

calm, all is bright. Round yon Vir – gin,

Moth – er and Child. Ho – ly in – fant so

ten – der and mild. Sleep in heav – en – ly pe –

ace, sle – ep in heav – en – ly pea – ce.

Level 1

Skip to My Lou

Children's song

When true sim – plic – i – ty is gain'd, to

bow and to bend we will not be a–sham'd, to

turn, turn will be our de – light, 'Till by

turn – ing, turn – ing we come 'round right.

The Farmer in the Dell

Children's song

♩ = 160

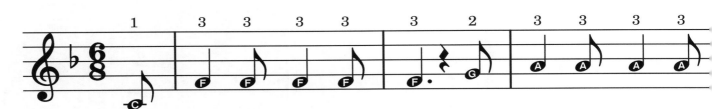

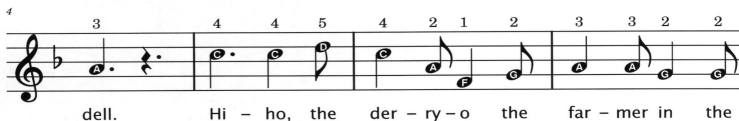

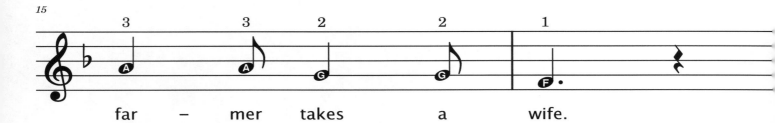

Level 1

The Muffin Man

Children's song

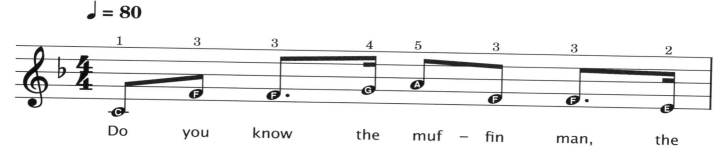

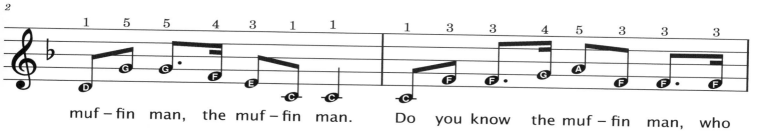

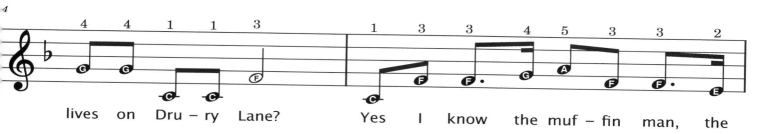

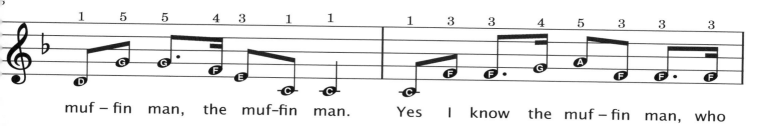

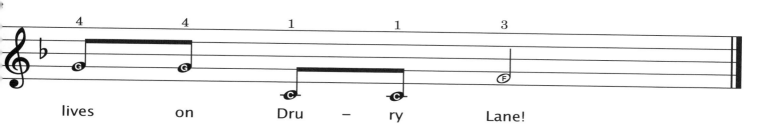

Video

Audio

Level 1

This Little Light of Mine

Gospel song

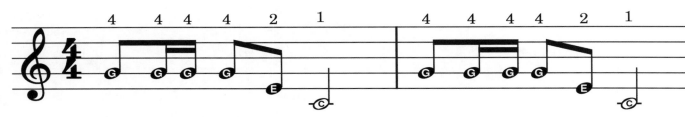

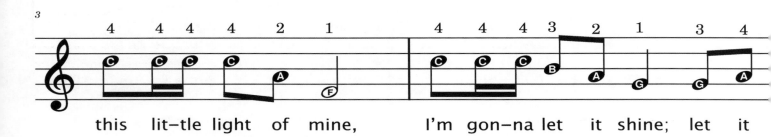

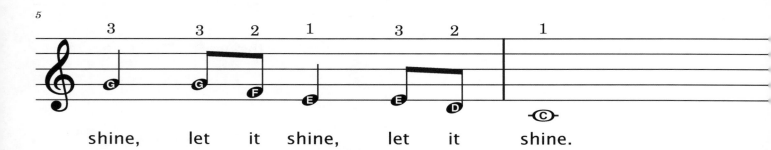

This Old Man

Children's song

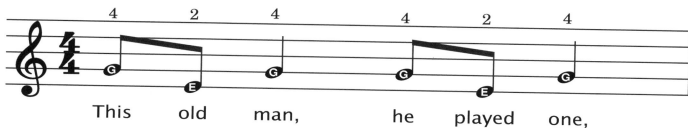

This old man, he played one,

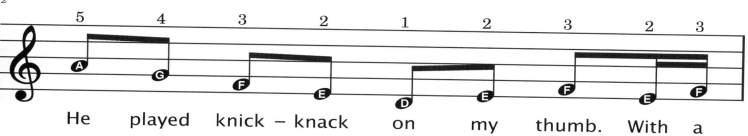

He played knick – knack on my thumb. With a

knick – knack pad – dy–whack, give your dog a bone.

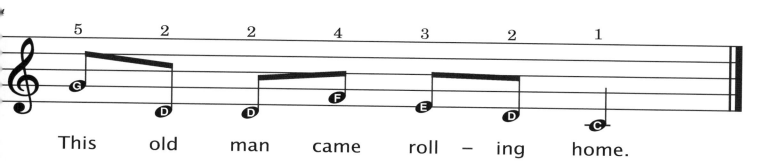

This old man came roll – ing home.

Level 1

Twinkle, Twinkle, Little Star

Children's song

♩ = 120

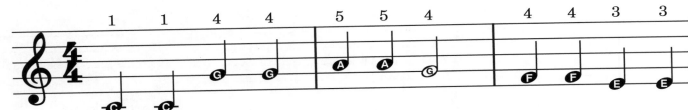

Twin – kle, twin – kle, lit – tle star, how I won–der

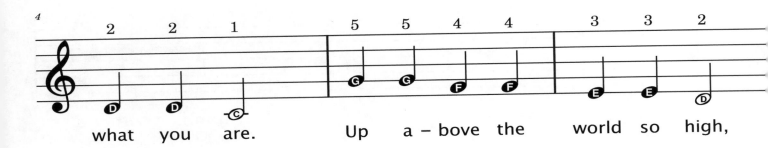

what you are. Up a – bove the world so high,

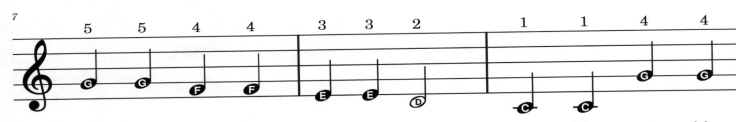

like a dia –mond in the sky. Twin – kle, twin – kle,

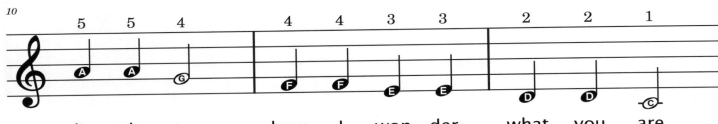

lit – tle star, how I won–der what you are.

Yankee Doodle

Children's song

Audio

Video

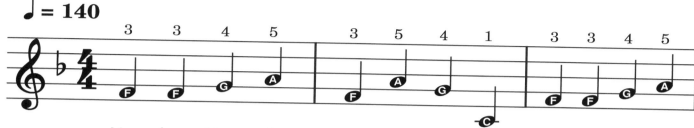

Yan – kee Doo – dle went to town, a – rid–ing on a

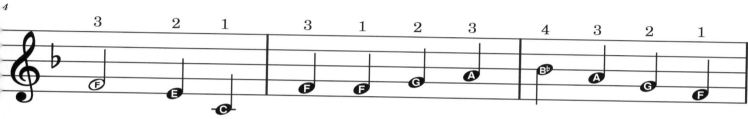

po – ny. He stuck a feath – er in his hat and

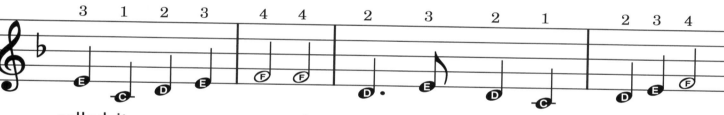

called it mac–a – ro – ni. Yan – kee Doo – dle, keep it up!

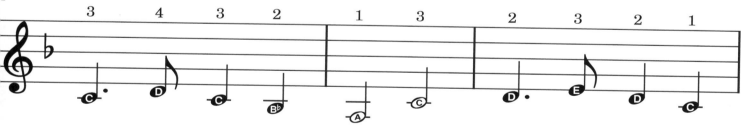

Yan – kee Doo – dle dan – dy! Mind the mu – sic

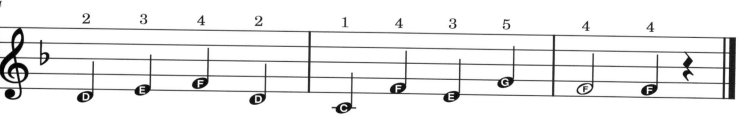

and the step, and with the girls be han – dy!

We Wish You A Merry Christmas

Christmas carol

Audio

Video

A-Tisket, A-Tasket

Children's song

Audio

Video

♩ = 100

All Through the Night

Christmas carol

Audio

Video

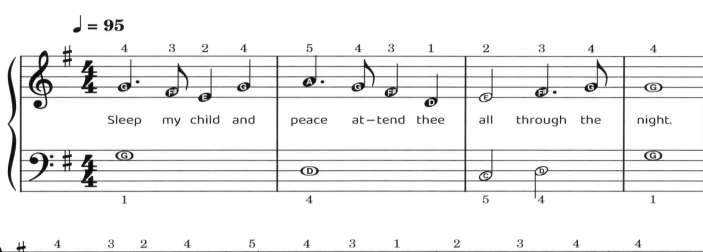

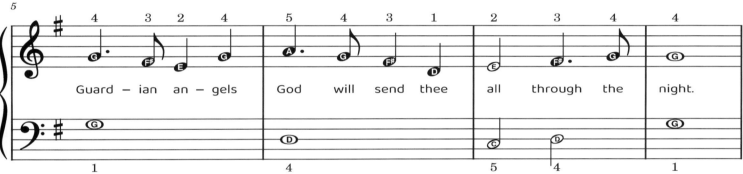

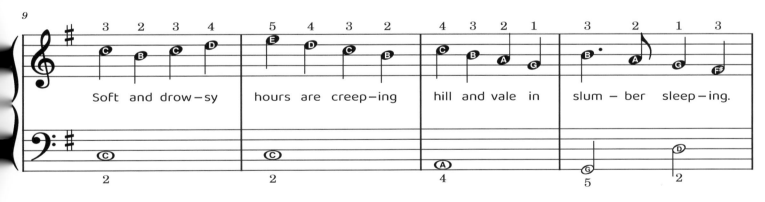

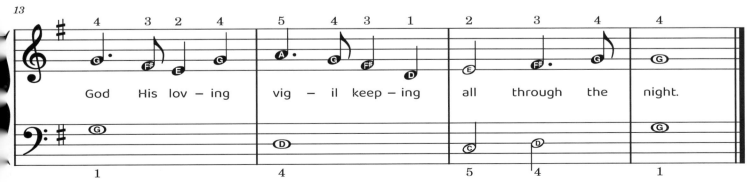

Alphabet Song

Children's song

Level 2

Amazing Grace

Christian hymn

49

Baa Baa Black Sheep

Children's song

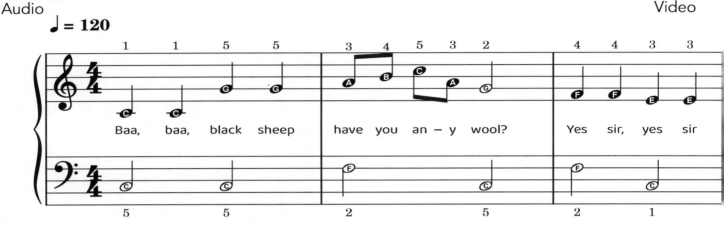

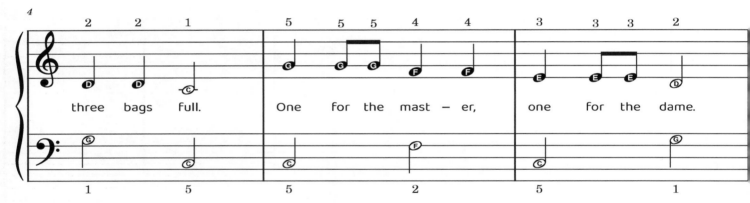

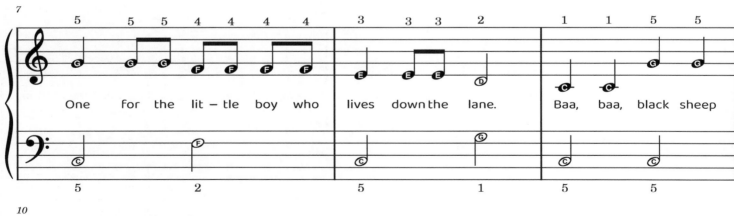

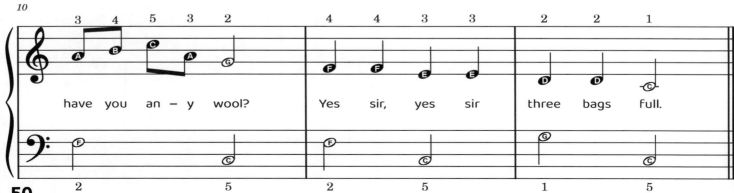

Billy Boy

Children's song

Audio

Video

O – oh, where have you been, Bil – ly Boy, Bil – ly Boy? O – oh,

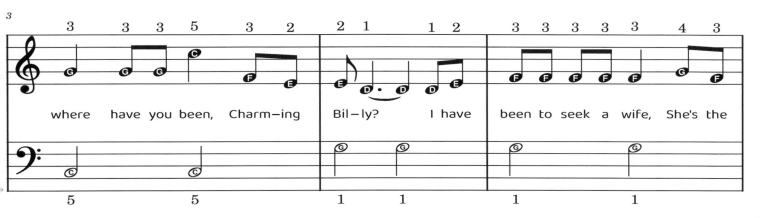

where have you been, Charm–ing Bil–ly? I have been to seek a wife, She's the

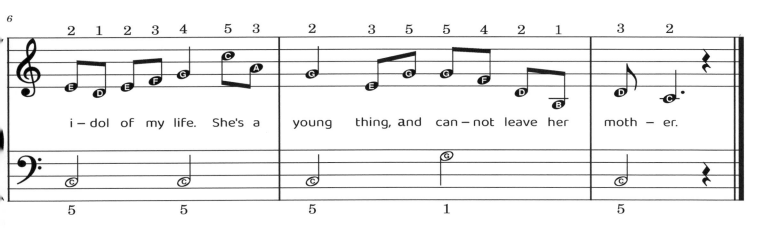

i – dol of my life. She's a young thing, and can – not leave her moth – er.

Level 2

Bingo

Children's song

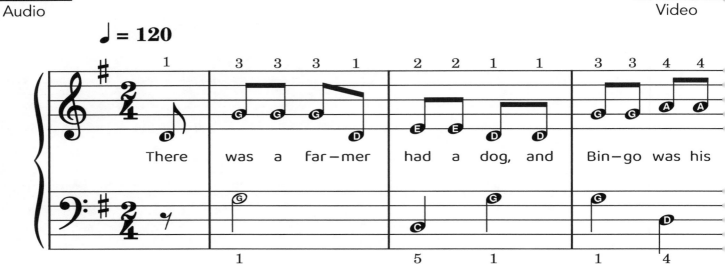

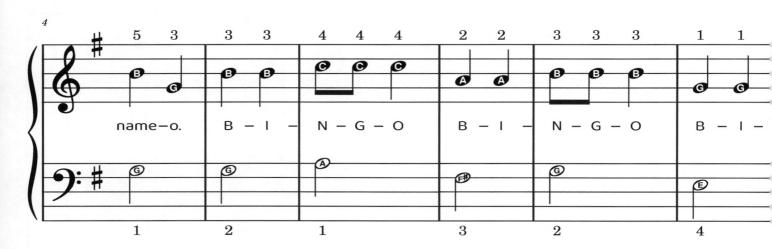

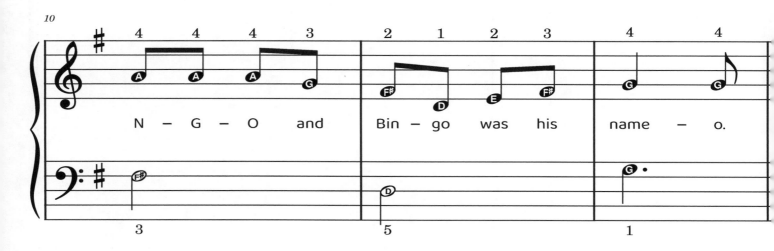

Brother John

Children's song

Audio

Video

♩ = 120

Are you | slee – ping are you | slee – ping Bro – ther | John? Bro — ther | John? Mor – ning bells are | ring — ing, mor – ning bells are | ring – ing Ding Ding | Dong Ding Ding | Dong.

Level 2

Clementine (Oh, My Darling)

Children's song

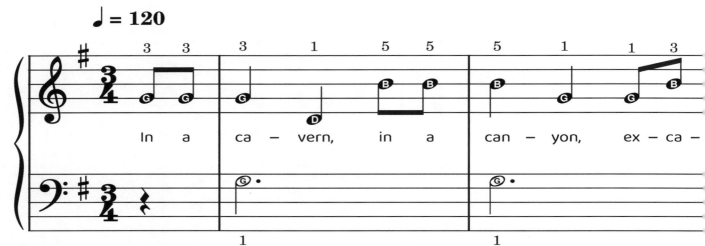

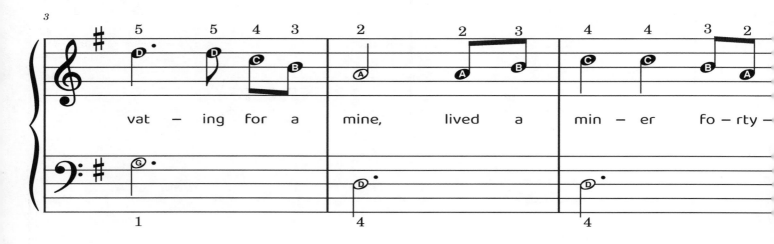

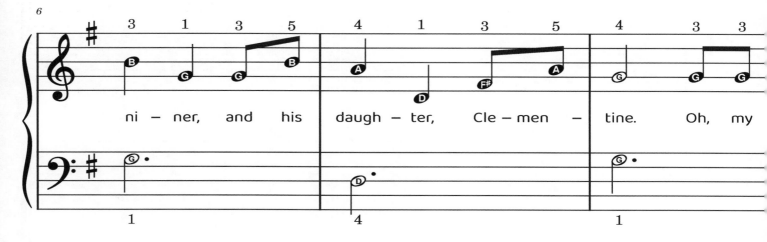

dar – ling, oh, my dar – ling, oh, my dar – ling Cle – men

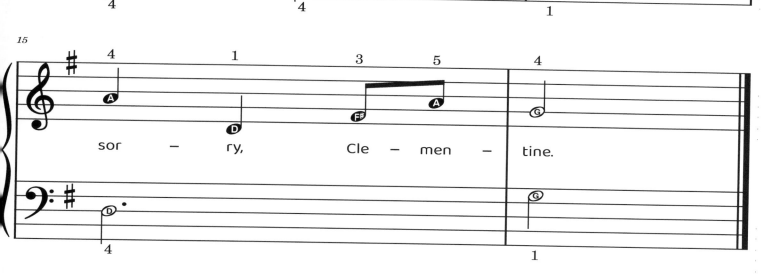

tine, — you are lost and gone for – ev – er, dread – ful

sor – ry, Cle – men – tine.

Greensleeves

English Folk Song

Audio

Georgie Porgie

Children's song

Video

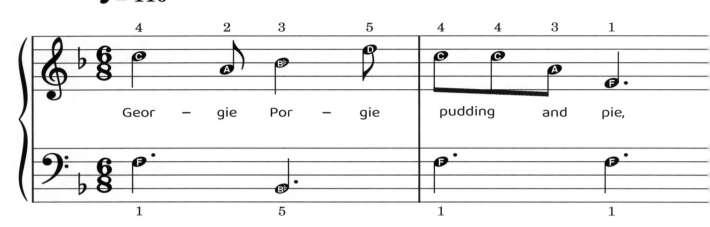

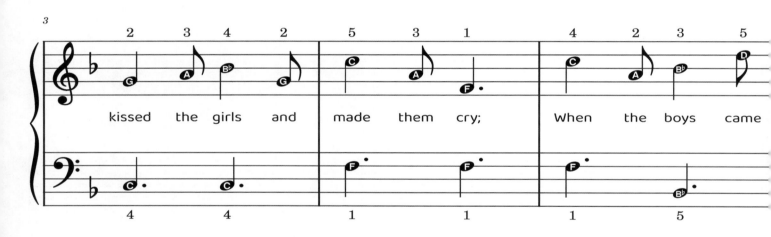

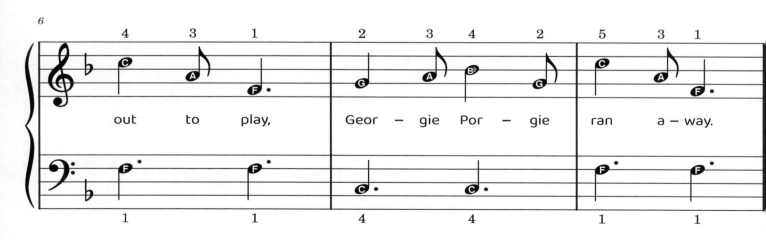

Level 2

Happy Birthday

Traditional song

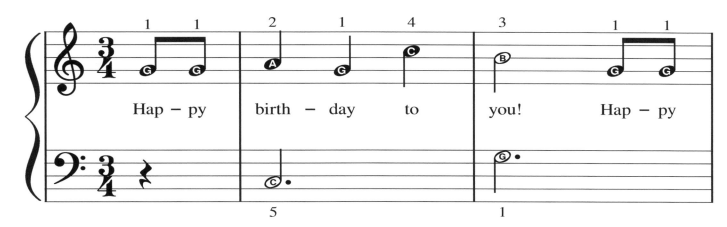

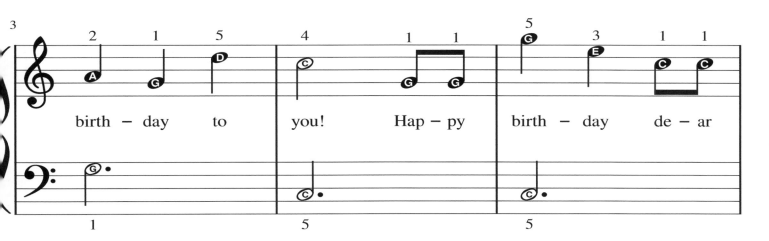

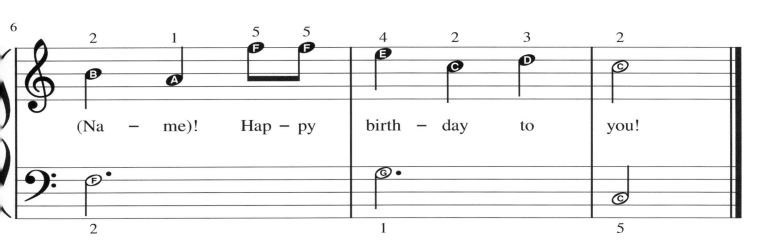

Hickory Dickory Dock

Children's song

Audio

Video

♩ = 120

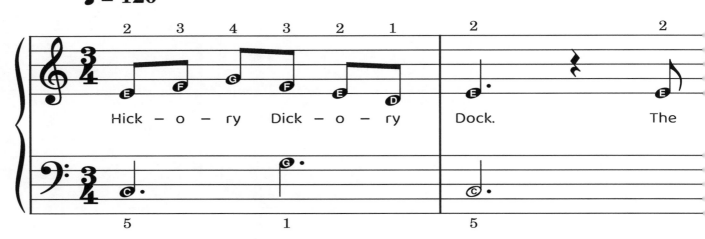

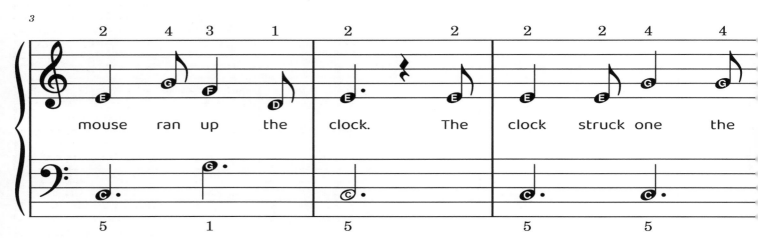

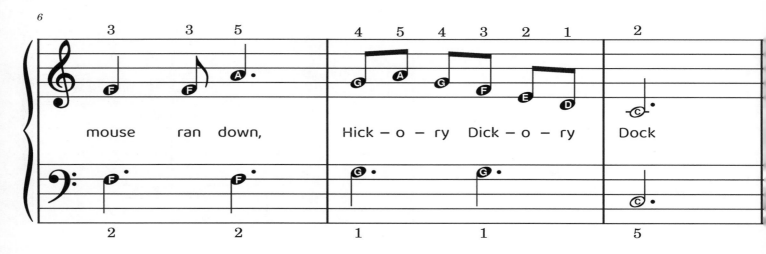

Level 2

Humpty Dumpty

Children's song

Audio

Video

$\bullet = 110$

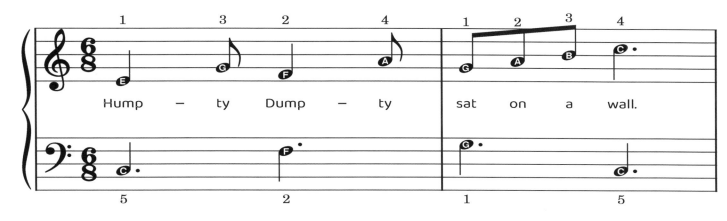

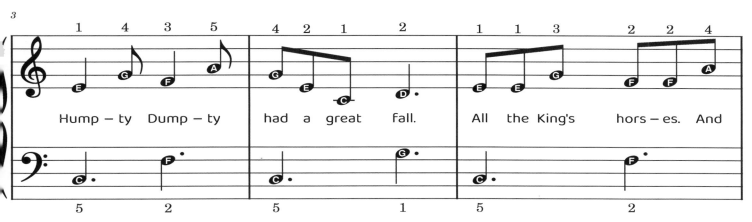

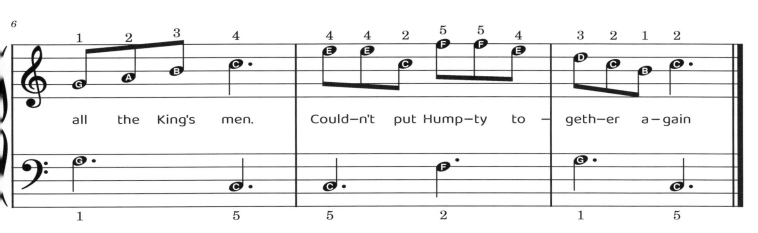

Hush, Little Baby

Children's song

Video

♩ = 110

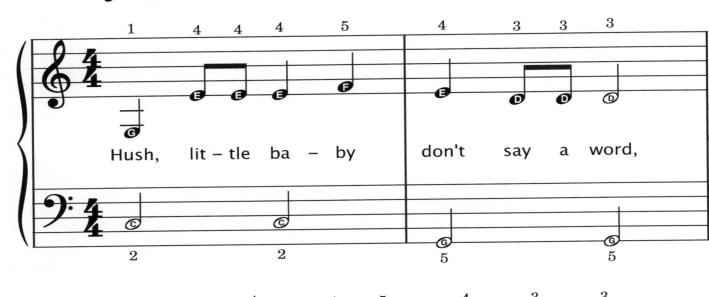

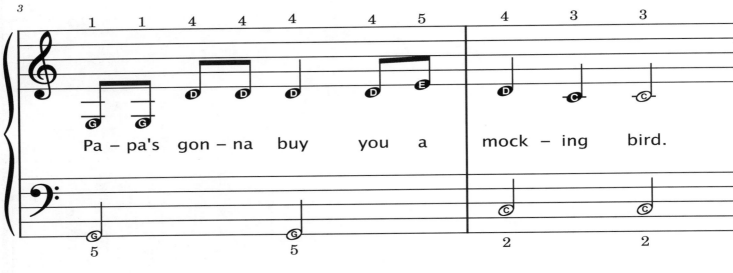

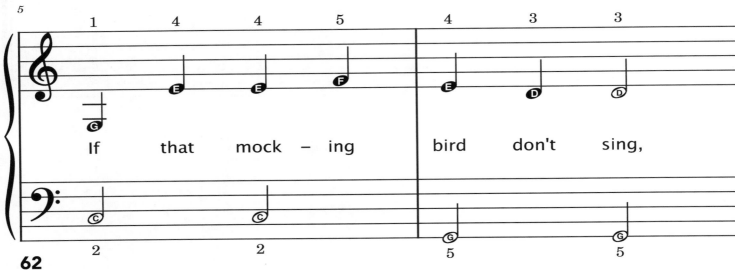

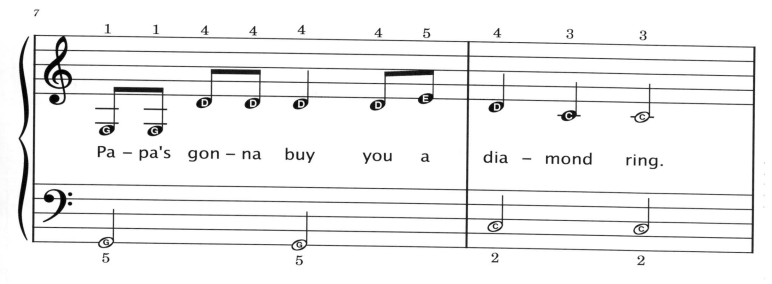

Pa – pa's gon – na buy you a dia – mond ring.

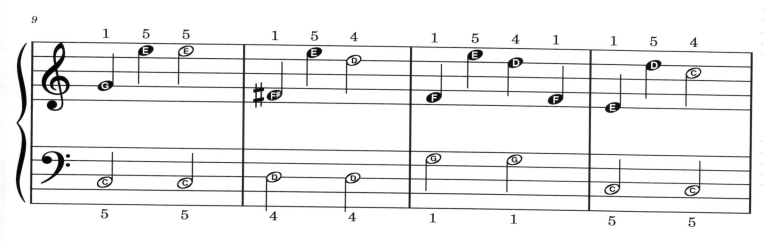

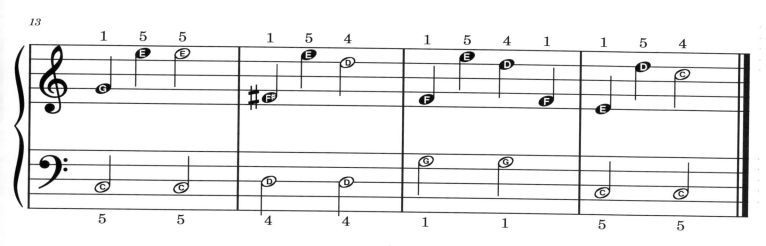

London Bridge

Children's song

Audio

Video

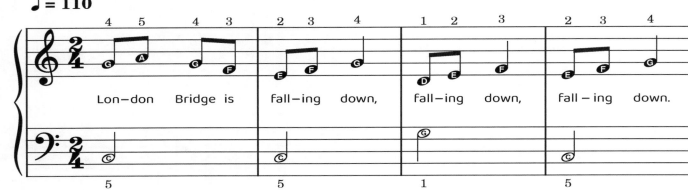

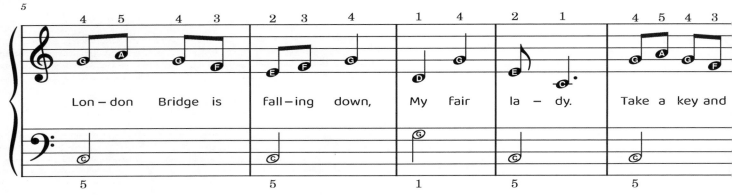

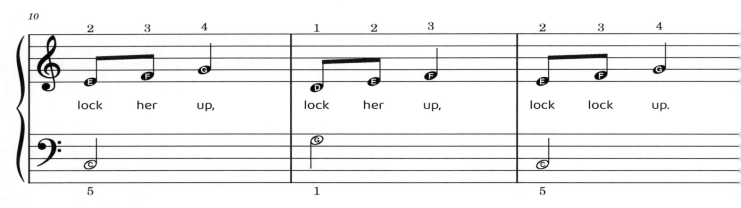

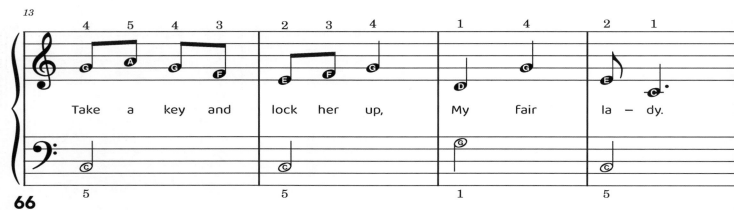

Mary Had a Little Lamb

Children's song

Audio

Video

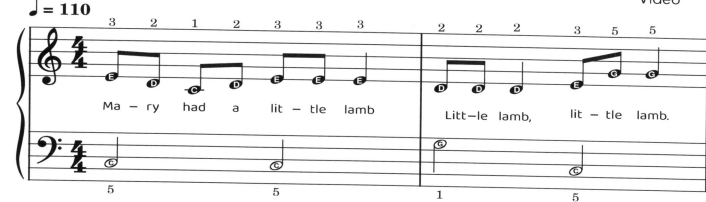

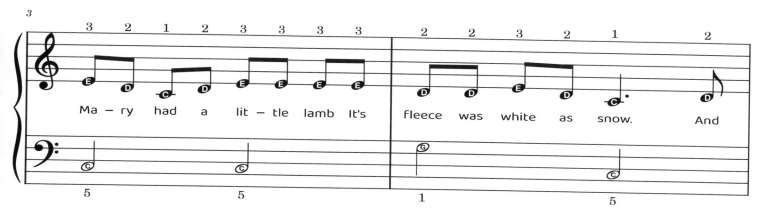

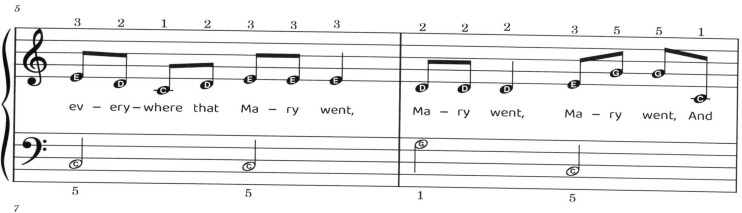

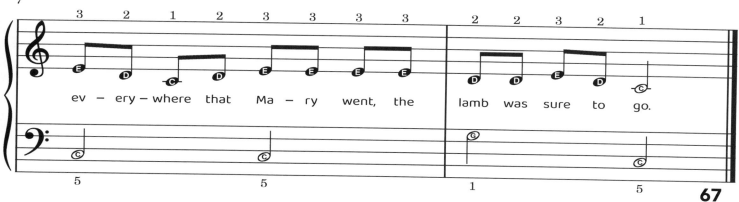

My Bonnie Lies Over The Ocean

Children's song

Audio

Video

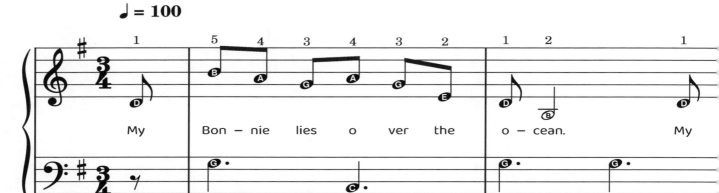

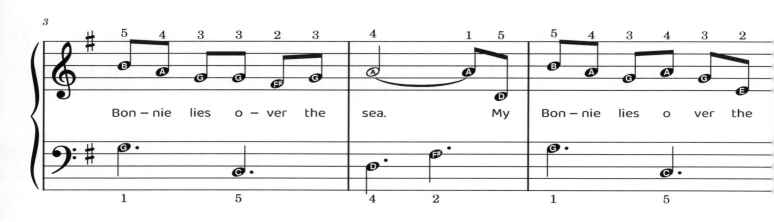

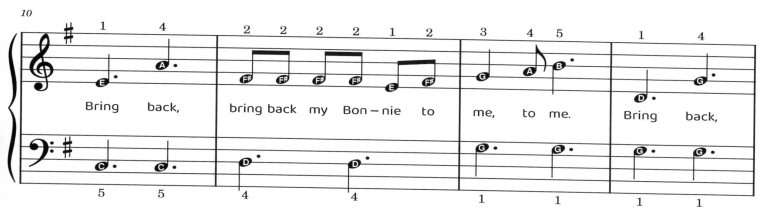

Bring back, bring back my Bon—nie to me, to me. Bring back,

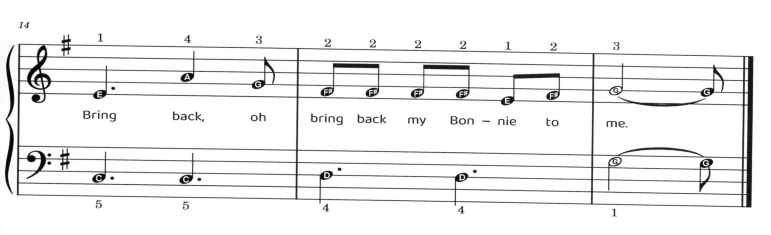

Bring back, oh bring back my Bon — nie to me.

O When The Saints

Christian hymn

Audio

Video

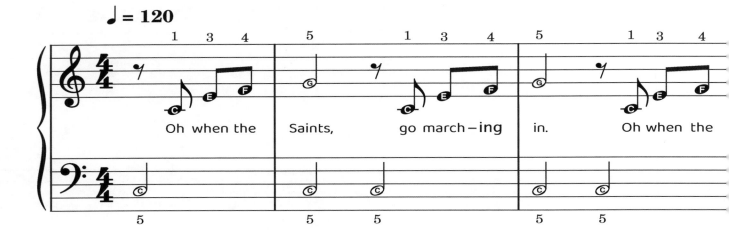

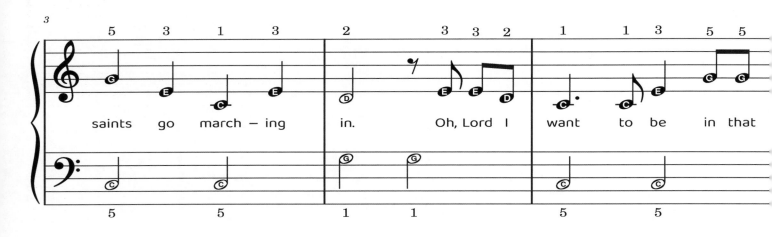

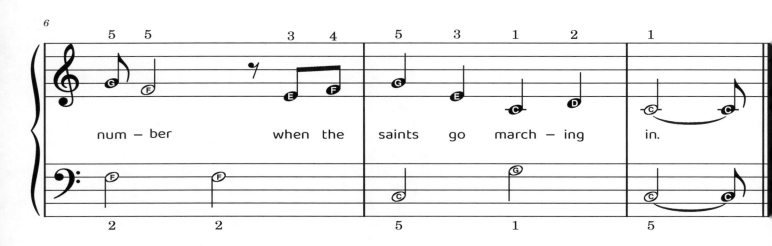

Old MacDonald Had a Farm

Children's song

Audio

Video

Pop! Goes the Weasel

Children's song

Audio

Video

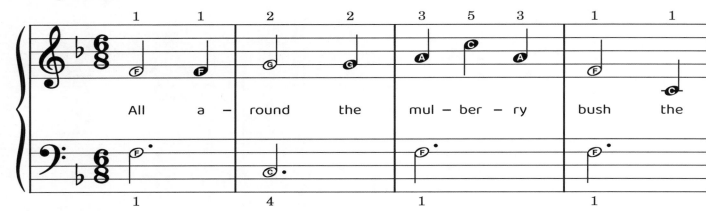

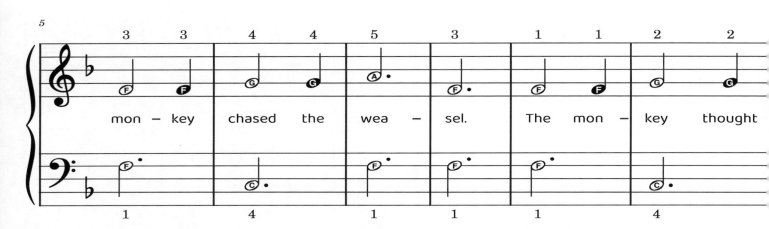

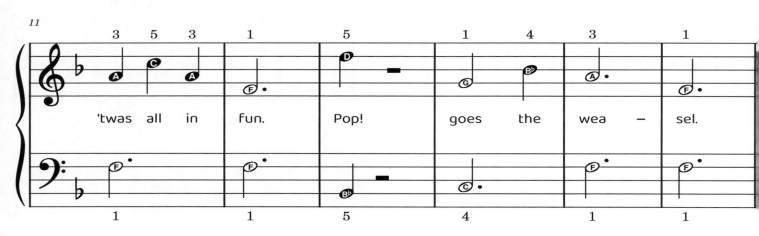

Audio

Pussy Cat, Pussy Cat

Children's song

Video

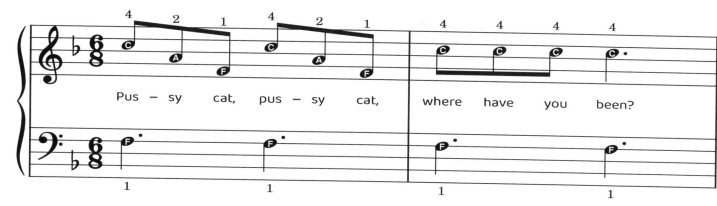

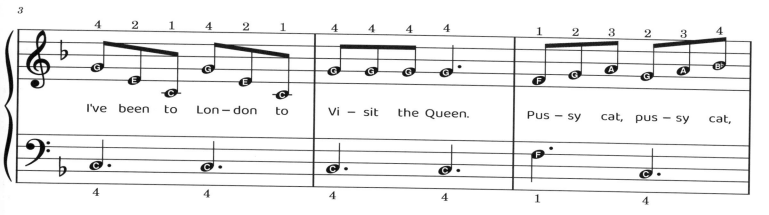

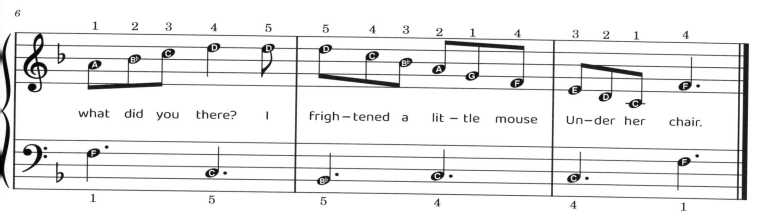

Rain, Rain, Go Away

Children's song

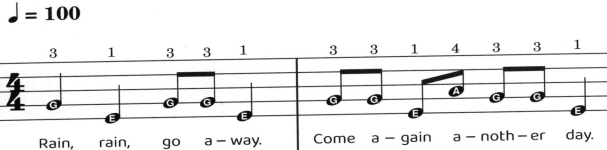

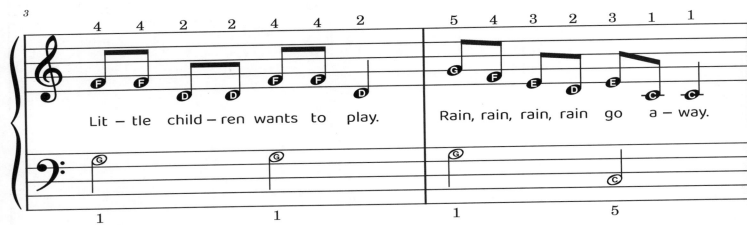

Level 2

Shenandoah

American Folk Song

♩ = 80

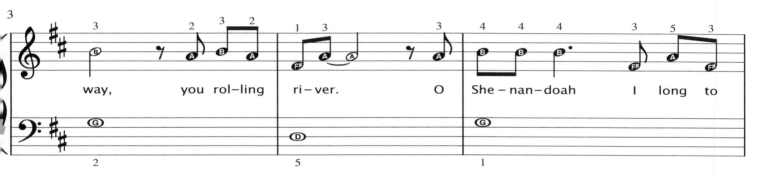

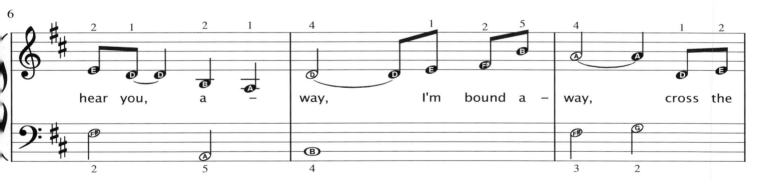

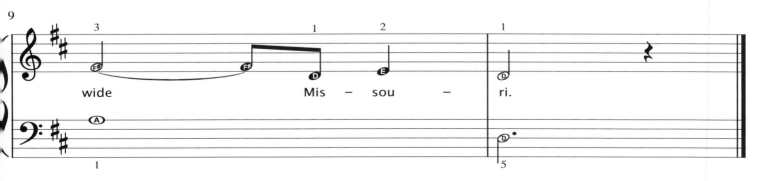

Silent Night

Christmas carol

Video

Audio

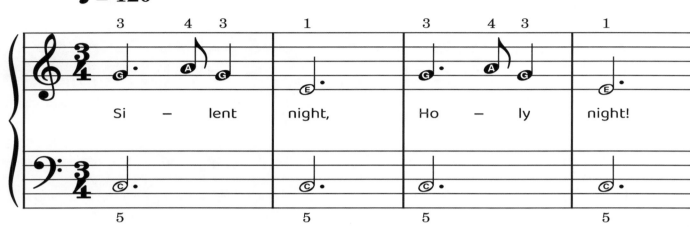

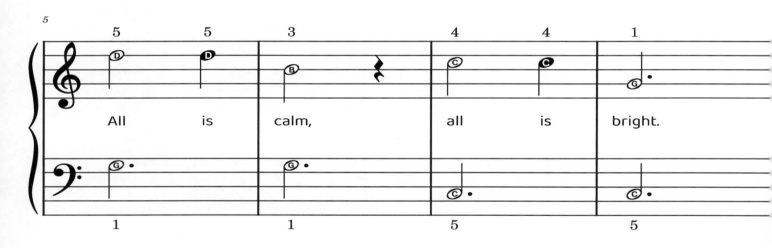

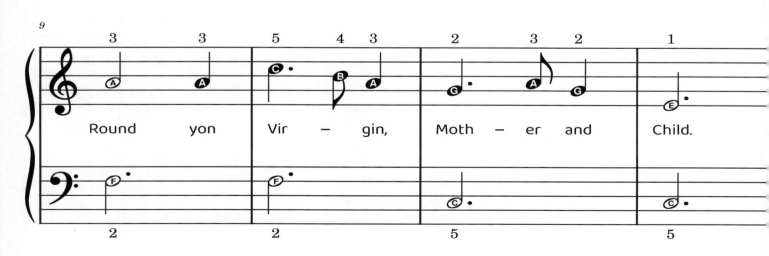

76

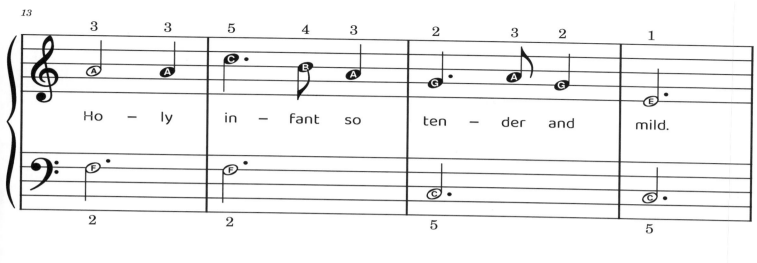

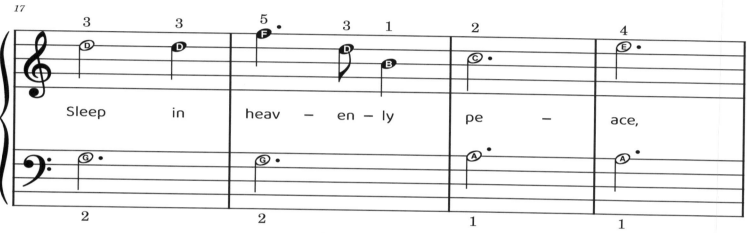

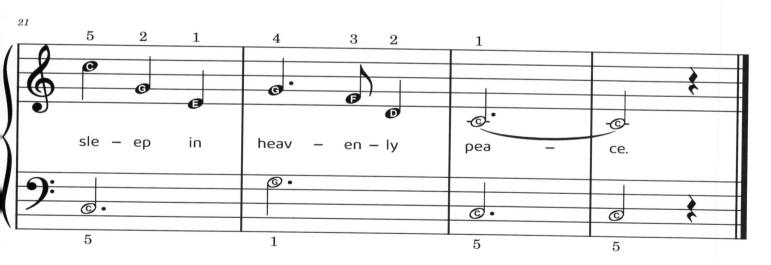

Level 2

Simple Gifts

Christian song

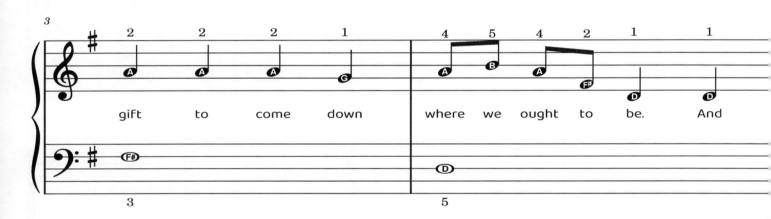

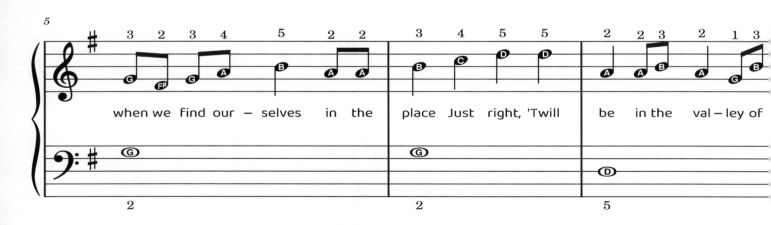

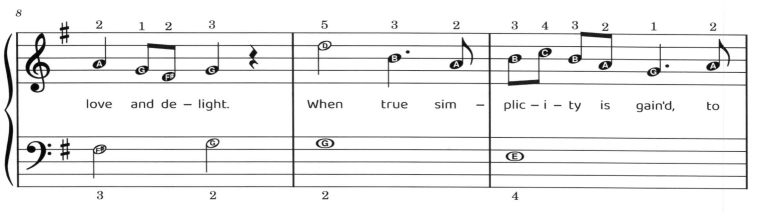

love   and   de – light.   When   true   sim —   plic – i – ty   is   gain'd,   to

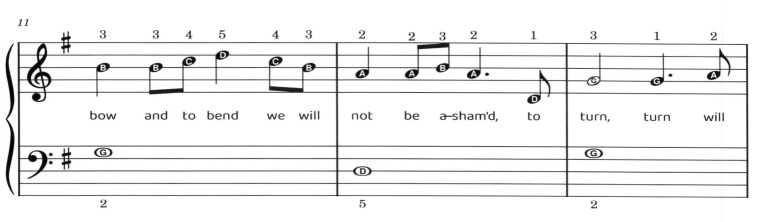

bow   and   to   bend   we   will   not   be   a–sham'd,   to   turn,   turn   will

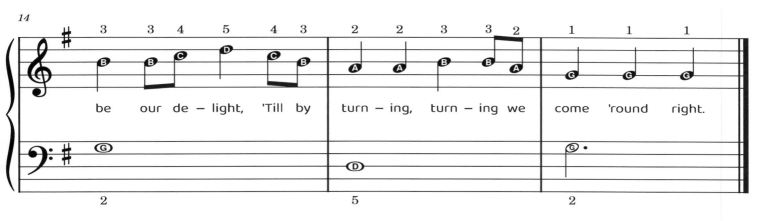

be   our   de – light, 'Till   by   turn – ing,   turn – ing   we   come   'round   right.

Skip to My Lou

Children's song

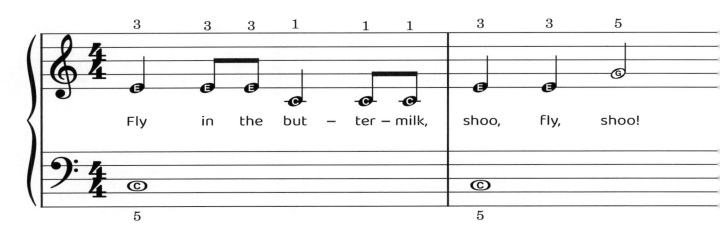

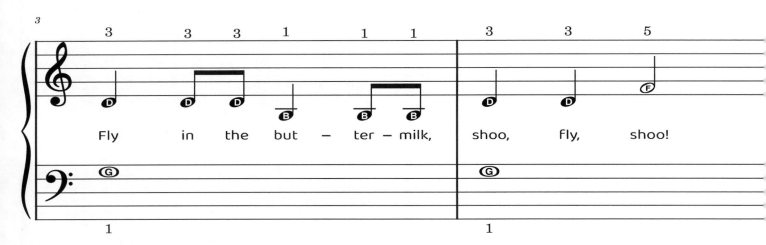

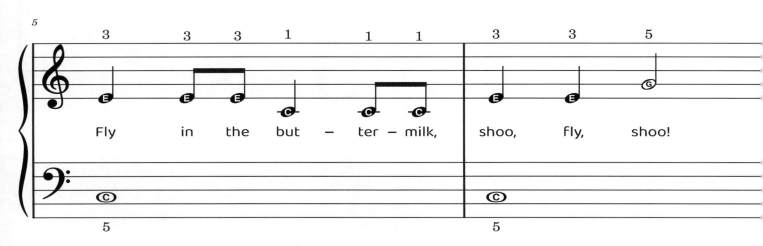

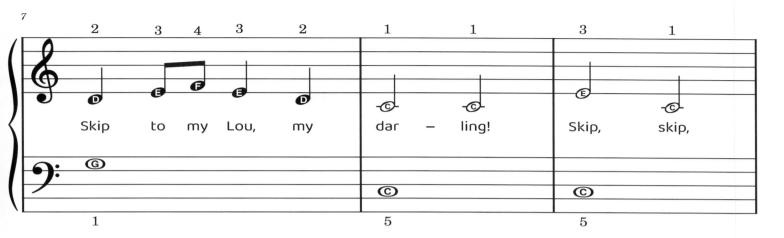

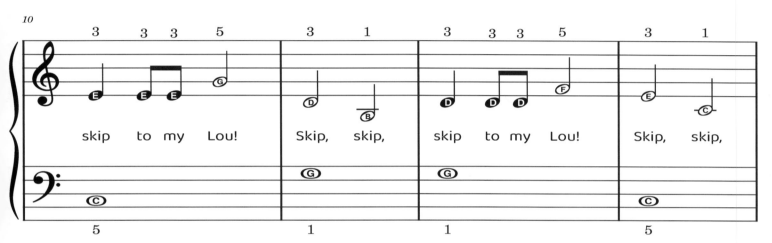

Audio

Level 2

The Farmer in the Dell

Children's song

Video

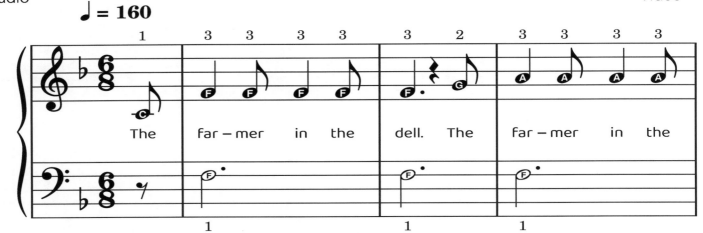

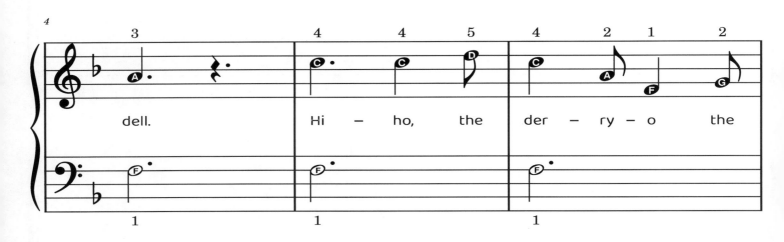

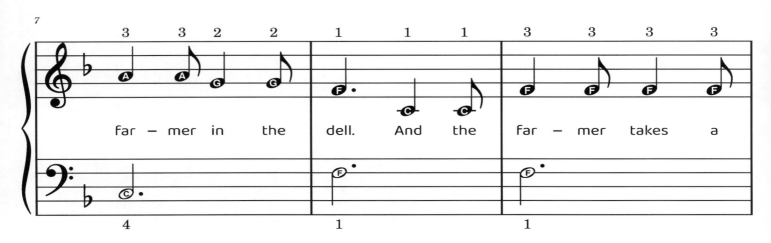

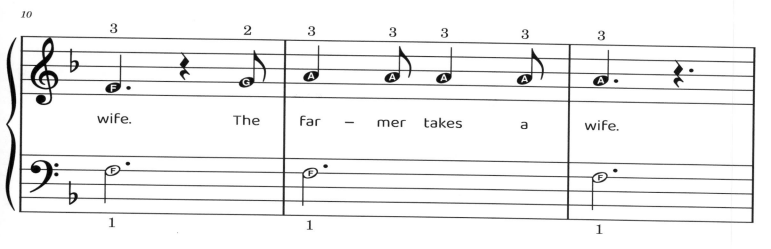

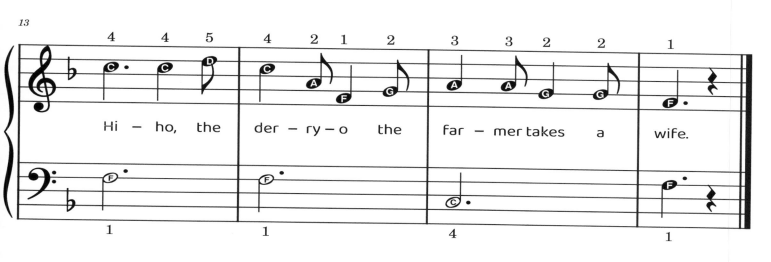

The Muffin Man

Children's song

Audio · Video

Level 2

This Little Light of Mine

Gospel song

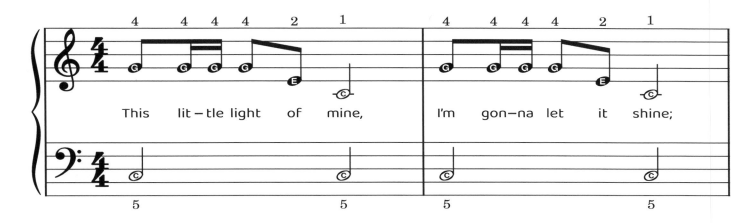

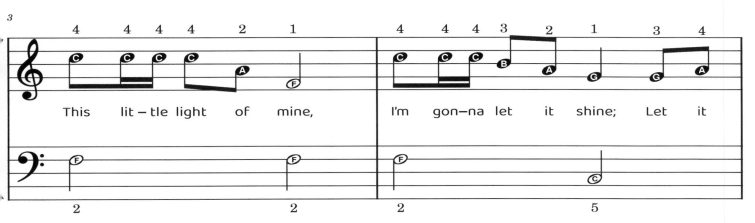

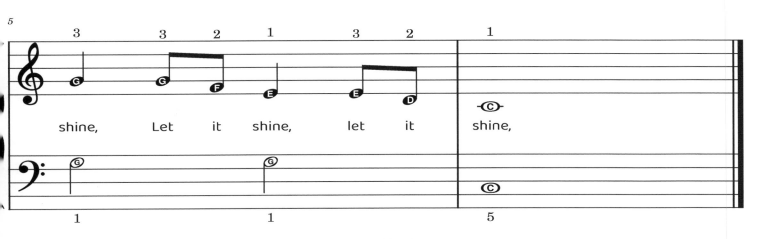

This Old Man

Children's song

Video

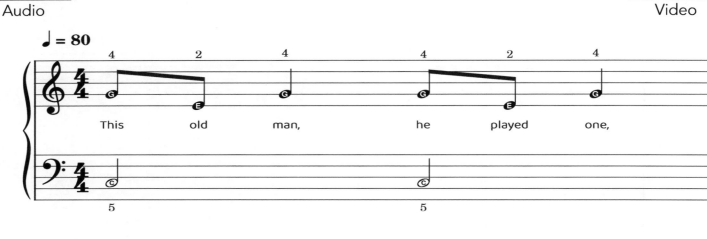

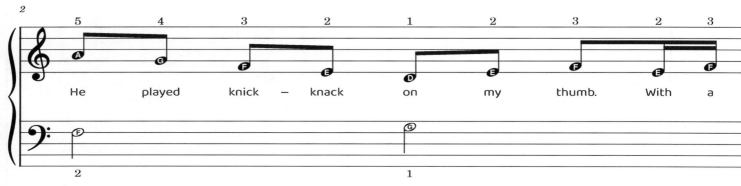

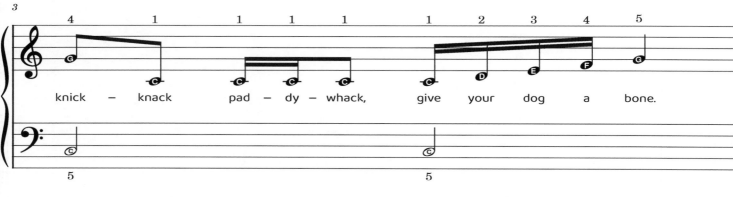

Twinkle, Twinkle, Little Star

Children's song

Audio

Video

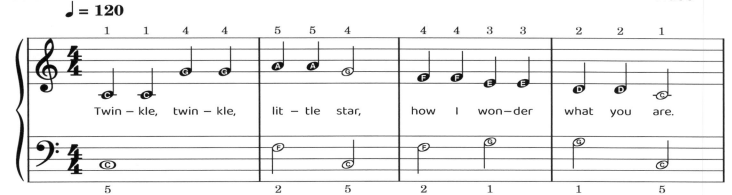

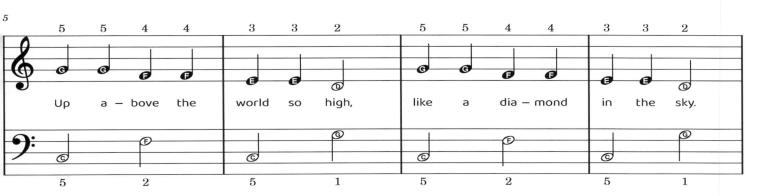

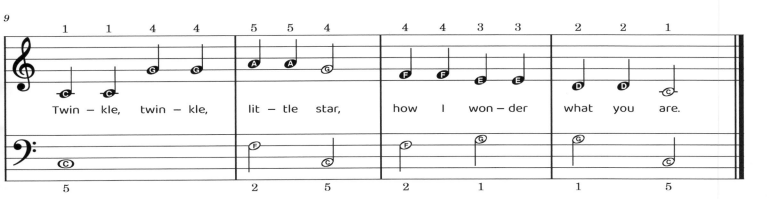

Audio

We Wish You A Merry Christmas

Christmas carol

Video

♩ = 120

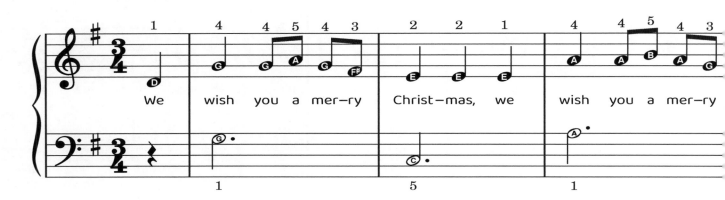

We wish you a mer—ry Christ—mas, we wish you a mer—ry

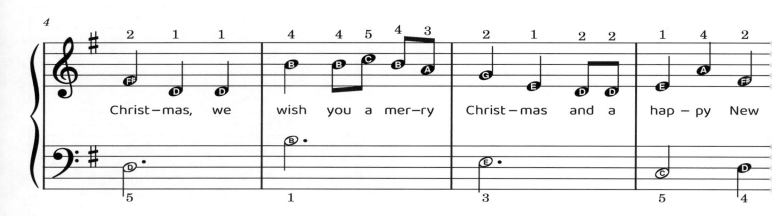

Christ—mas, we wish you a mer—ry Christ—mas and a hap—py New

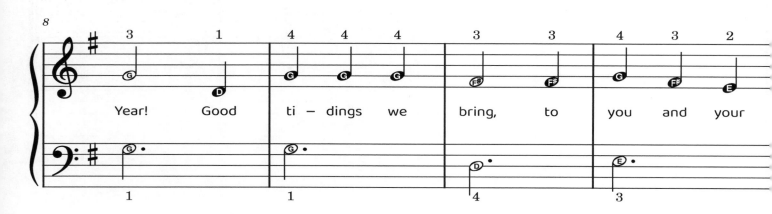

Year! Good ti—dings we bring, to you and your

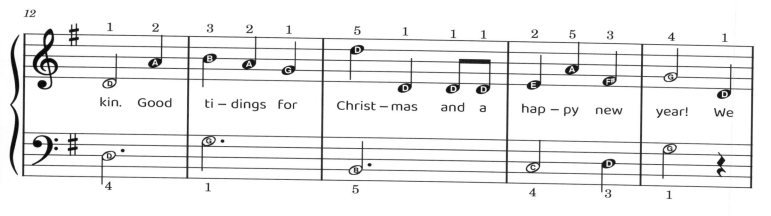

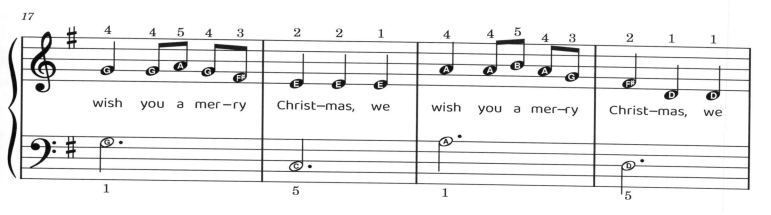

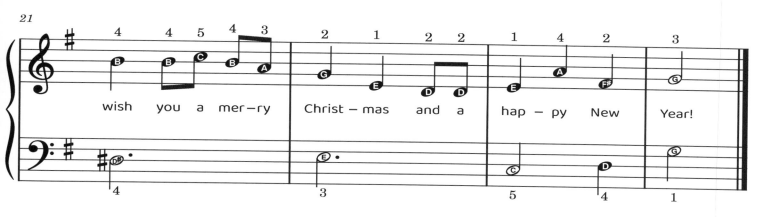

Level 2

Yankee Doodle

Children's song

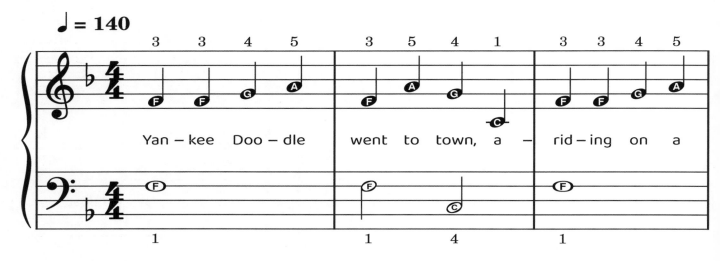

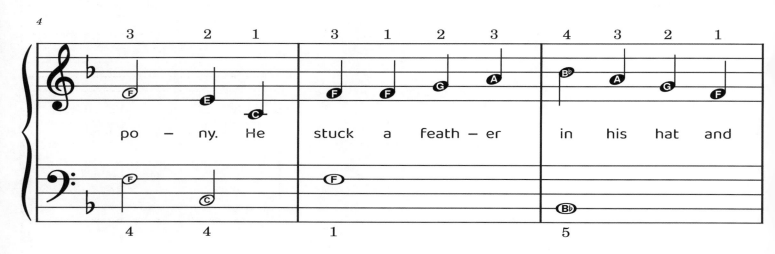

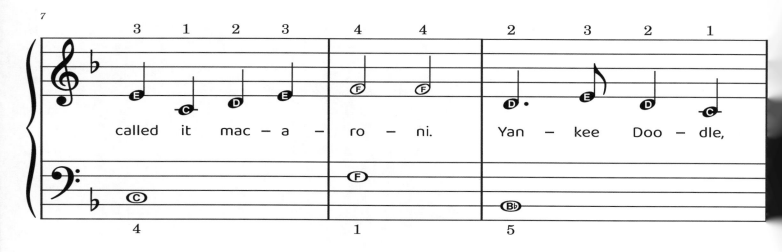

online review

Thank you for your recent purchase. We hope you will love it! If you can, would you consider posting an **online review on Amazon**? This will help us continue to provide great products and help potential buyers make confident decisions.

Thank you in advance for your review and for being a preferred customer.

online review

QR & Links*

All Audio Files (on Google Drive)

You are about to be redirected to another page.

Redirect in 15   Go back

You are about to be redirected to another page. We are not responsible for the content of that page or the consequences it may have on you.

https://goo-gl.me/ngOmp (this is an abbreviated link)
https://drive.google.com/drive/folders/1ZskzbsO0qVerfDgK0TsgEoRVxR91djac?usp=drive_link **(full link)**

All Print Files (on Google Drive)

https://goo-gl.me/3l43q (this is an abbreviated link)
https://drive.google.com/drive/folders/15PIzF-BcURbBbOV7CG5HY73zsALQsMYk?usp=sharing **(full link)**

All Video Files (on YouTube)

https://goo-gl.me/v0hLg (this is an abbreviated link)
youtube.com/playlist?list=PLD9E7uLFX4pxM9bvSPwQAFNW1WgY5UOfK&si=92AzNLd0RptCqFgy **(full link)**

* If you have not received a bonus or you have questions, write suggestions here: help@paulterence.com

amazon.com/dp/B09ZG3W9CF

amazon.co.uk/dp/B09ZG3W9CF

amazon.ca/dp/B09ZG3W9CF

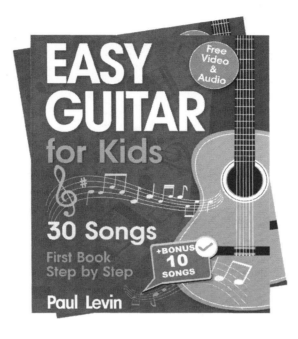

amazon.com/dp/B0C7J9D217

amazon.co.uk/dp/B0C7J9D217

amazon.ca/dp/B0C7J9D217

Made in the USA
Las Vegas, NV
14 January 2024

84366693R00052